I0549024

SMASH THE HAMMER

SMASH THE HAMMER

250-WORD STORIES

Sean Hill

SMASH THE HAMMER
250-Word Stories

Published by
SMASH THE HAMMER
www.smashthehammer.com

Edited by Troy A. Miller
www.troyanthonymiller.com

The author greatly appreciates you taking the time to read his work. Please consider leaving a review wherever you bought the book, or telling your friends or blog readers about Smash The Hammer, to help spread the word. Thanks for your support.

Visit the website and blog of
Sean Hill at www.seanhill.com

DEDICATION

Rae Rae, this book is for you.

You stepped into my life bearing a tray of brownies - all good muses come with chocolate.

PRAISE FOR
VERY SHORT STORIES:
300-BITE SIZE WORKS OF FICTION
by Sean Hill

"Hilarious Stories"
>   - Huffington Post

"Some are touching, some ring true, but most are laugh-out-loud funny."
>   - Seattle Times

"The book is a treasure-trove of fascinating exploration into the craft of language and storytelling."
>   - Summit Daily

"Story telling is his bag, pure and simple"
>   - Austin American Statesman

"The best of the stories might rival Hemingway's classic six word story in their descriptive brevity and their ability to tell a complete and affecting tale."
>   - Short and Sweet NYC

"Witty, well-crafted and always thought-provoking."
>   - Salt Lake Tribune

"Celebrating brevity, precision, and the art of subtle communication, author Sean Hill has crafted hundreds of engaging, evocative stories that conjure up an entire novel in a sentence or two."
>   - ITGawker

PRAISE FOR
@VERYSHORTSTORY
by Sean Hill

"These are great! I'm hooked!"
- @RainnWilson

"These are the only tweets I have sent directly to my phone."
- @DitaVonTeese

"You pack more emotion, meaning, and plot twists into 140 characters then most authors do in a novel."
- @WintersNight

"If you haven't discovered @VeryShortStory, check it out. Brilliant twitter-sized fiction."
- @PrettyLittleBan

"@VeryShortStory Builds a picture in your mind, that just grows."
- @QBlicious

"Flash fiction at its best"
- @Taquinmontreau

"Amazing stories (with a beginning, middle, and end) in less than 140 characters."
- @ClayRivers

"The best stories you'll ever read in 140 characters or less. EVER!"
- @Zecois

INTRODUCTION

For a few years I've been writing 140-character stories on Twitter under my @VeryShortStory account where I have over 100,000 daily readers. It's been a satisfying creative outlet for me and the readers there have been wonderfully supportive.

Those readers often ask where they can read some longer stories of mine. Well, here is your chance. I've written fifty 250-word stories for this collection so you can get your fix.

These stories are short enough to fit on a single page but lengthy enough that I can put in details that don't fit in my 140-character stories. I had fun writing them and I hope they amuse and entertain you.

I appreciate your taking the time to read my work. Please consider leaving a review wherever you bought the book, or telling your friends or blog readers about Smash The Hammer, to help spread the word.

Thanks,
Sean

Connect with me online:

WEBSITE
www.seanhill.com

TWITTER
twitter.com/sean_hill

FACEBOOK
facebook.com/sean.hill.writer

LINKEDIN
linkedin.com/in/veryshortstory

Harmony

Mike and Sarah struggled in their relationship. There were so many things they had a difference of opinion about. These differences were a source of constant friction.

One Saturday morning, after a big Friday night fight, Sarah saw the ad in the paper: "No more disagreements. Bring harmony to your relationship."

"Harmony," Sarah said. That was it. That was what she wanted. She loved Mike. In that moment, she was sure of it more than ever. What she desperately wanted with Mike was harmony.

Sarah showed Mike the ad. He held it in his hands and started to cry. "Harmony," he said. "I want that." Mike put down the paper and hugged Sarah. It was the first real hug they'd shared in quite a while.

The next day they went together to the address listed in the ad. It was a small office at 232 Duncan Street. It had a bright blue door with a small sign that read "Harmony, Inc. Dr. Robert Theopolis".

Mike and Sarah sat on the couch in the waiting room, each of them feeling a little scared.

"Harmony," Sarah said.

"Harmony," Mike replied, grasping her hand.

They met with Dr. Theopolis. After reading his brochure, they agreed this is what they wanted. They wrote out a check for his services. They would start the process right away.

The operation was a success. Dr. Theopolis linked Mike and Sarah's brains, forming one mind, one set of thoughts. The constant friction was gone; there was only harmony.

Sometimes

Sometimes there is nothing to say. This was one of those moments. I'd just watched you fall 400 feet off the side of the cliff. I was still holding a glass of champagne in my hand. A moment before, I had been trying to hand it to you. When I turned around and held it out, I'd bumped you in the back, causing your long descent.

I was surprised how long it takes someone to fall 400 feet. It seemed like an eternity as I watched you get smaller and smaller.

While you were falling, all kinds of thoughts raced through my head. The first thought was You're gonna be mad at me, then Do something! Go after her, followed by damn and the lingering That really didn't go as planned.

This was supposed to be the moment where we celebrated that I'd just proposed to you by drinking champagne together and looking out at the beautiful view.

I'd known for a while that you wanted me to propose. I waited until today because it seemed like the best birthday present I could give you.

I'd saved for months to afford the ring, checking with your girlfriends to make sure you'd like it. When I pulled it out of my pocket, you smiled and your eyes opened wide. I could tell you liked it. I hope the ring was some small comfort during your descent.

There was a tiny cloud of dust when you landed. Now there was nothing to say.

Cake Love

Smash The Hammer: 250-Word Stories

I'm not sure exactly when I fell in love with cake, somewhere during my childhood. Mom was never good with words or physical affection, but she made a hell of a cake.

It wasn't until I was older I figured out she was buying them instead of baking them; so really, she could buy a hell of a cake.

I never had a babysitter growing up. If Mom were going out for the night she would just leave a cake out for me on the kitchen table. I guess she figured that having a whole cake to eat would keep me out of trouble. And it did. It also kept me from ever having a girlfriend or learning about real affection.

I tried dating in college, but it never really went anywhere. I'd go to dinner with a girl. We'd chitchat awkwardly during the meal, then dessert would arrive. I'd lose interest in the girl and focus on the cake, enjoying every bite. It didn't lead to many second dates.

I tried breaking up with cake. Went a whole three weeks without talking to or touching a cake, but the loneliness was unbearable. It lead to an all out binge. When I woke up from my cake blackout, I was in bed, pieces of cake all around. Photos of the things we'd done the night before scattered everywhere.

Cake and I continue to spend time together, but now we have an open relationship. I've started seeing donuts too.

This Time Around

Smash The Hammer: 250-Word Stories

"Have you selected something from the menu?"

"I'm still thinking it over. Last time I had the Work Constantly, Make a lot of Money, Die Alone. It was ok, but I'm thinking of trying something different this time. How's that Perfect Life I saw listed on the specials board?"

"Unfortunately, we are all out of the Perfect Life. It was very popular today. We do have another special, the Super Famous Child Star, Over the Hill at 16."

"Hmmm…I don't think I'm really in the mood for that. You're sure there's no Perfect Life left?"

"Very sure. It went rather quickly."

"OK then, what about the Simple Life? Does that come with romance?"

"No, the Simple Life doesn't include any sides. If you want romance you might try the Third Time's a Charm."

"Oooh, tell me about that."

"You suffer through two horrible, disastrous marriages that break you emotionally and financially, then just when you're about to throw in the towel, you meet the love of your life. Comes with a side of children and a Springer spaniel."

"A Springer spaniel sounds nice. I think I'd like a dog."

"Many people do, but I should mention that one also comes with dog allergies. A lot of people are put off by that."

"Hmmm..,you know, I think I'm just gonna go with the Work Constantly, Make a lot of Money, Die Alone again. I feel more comfortable with that."

"Very well, this way please. We'll send you right down."

Jared

Jared sat alone in his bed, hugging his knees to his chest. His face rubbing against the soft flannel of the pajamas he was wearing. He glanced over at the clock on the nightstand, making sure it was still unplugged.

Before getting in bed, Jared had gone around his 10th floor apartment and unplugged anything that displayed the time; microwave, cable box, Mickey Mouse wall clock. He'd also pried open his watch, removed the batteries and thrown them in the trash.

Jared hoped that all the unplugging would keep it from happening. So far, it seemed to be working. Although with no clocks to check, he couldn't be sure. But he hadn't heard any fireworks or people shouting "Happy New Year" in the hall.

Just last week, Jared's life had been more carefree. He spent his nights out with friends laughing and having a good time.

That was until his friend Amy dragged him to see a fortune-teller. Not really Jared's type of thing, but when a red headed, big-boobed woman you want to sleep with invites you to go somewhere, you go.

The next morning, Jared woke up to a tiny beeping coming from his desk drawer. He walked over to the desk and opened the drawer. There was an old forgotten watch, flashing the time and date: 7:00am 01/01.

Jared started crying. The fortune-teller had said that this year would be his last, and it would…although it was just a lucky guess.

Your Birthday

I snuck out of the office early, excited to go home and share your birthday with you. I wanted to make it special this year. I picked up yellow roses, your favorite, and headed home.

All week I'd thought about what you would want as a gift. Then it hit me; you would want some time with me. Recently at work, I overheard someone saying, "The most valuable thing you can give someone is your time."

So that's what I did. I planned an evening to give you my time. I would just be with you. A fancy dinner at La Mont, a moonlight drive to the top of the hills where we would hold hands and talk as we looked out at the view over the city. Then to make it really special, instead of taking you home, we would pull up to the Hotel Walters and check in to an elaborate suite.

When I got home, the house was quiet and peaceful. I found you upstairs in the tub. Candles and bubbles all around. You looked just as beautiful as the day we met.

"Happy Birthday," I said, showing you the flowers. You smiled.

I undressed to join you and slid into the opposite end of the tub.

That's when I noticed the two champagne glasses sitting on the edge of the tub, already empty. I looked at you.

"Now!" you yelled. I heard the closet door jerk open then something smashed down on the back of my head.

Slave Wanted

My love life had drifted into the fog. The lovemaking with Kim had become robotic. Gone were the towering heights of passion. Sex had become boring, something I hadn't thought was possible.

How did it get this way? Was it like this for everyone? Is it inevitable that love and sex become mundane when the excitement wears off?

I sprinkled sugar into the foam of my double café mocha and let those thoughts turn over in my mind. That's when I noticed the ad pinned on the bulletin board next to me. "Slave wanted. No experience necessary. Call Sheila 598-2349."

Something stirred inside of me. My mind created pictures of me bound in leather, with a beautiful dominatrix dripping hot candle wax across my chest as she forced me to do her bidding.

That was it. It wasn't sex that had become boring; it was Kim. What I needed was a partner who was exciting. Exciting partner equals exciting sex. Things were becoming clear.

Later that day, I rang Sheila's doorbell ready for adventure. She opened the door. She was a looker, on the top-side of fifty, but well put together with long blonde hair and a pretty smile.

We went inside and sat on the couch in her living room. "So how do we get started?" I asked.

"Clean this room first, then I have some tile work for you to do in the kitchen."

Turned out Sheila was celibate, but needed a lot of chores done.

My Collection

I first saw Bess in the flower store standing behind the counter. She was absolutely stunning. A work of art as pretty as the flowers she was tending.

Speaking with her about the variety of roses in the shop, I took in her every movement. Her responses showed her to be quite intelligent with charm to match her beauty. Like a rare gem, I found her flawless.

After purchasing flowers, I invited Bess out to my estate for the Black and White Ball on Saturday night.

The Black and White Ball was an annual event where I invited a select crowd into my home and displayed a few of the exquisite pieces I had collected over the previous year. The center piece of that year's collection was a diamond covered piano formerly belonging to the late King of Siam.

I saw Bess from across the room and my pulse quickened. She hadn't resisted my invitation. I waited a few moments then went over to greet her.

"Good evening," I said.

"Good evening. Your home is quite remarkable."

"Thank you. Come with me, let me show you around."

I held my arm out and she took it. Together we walked through the house as I explained about each treasure we passed.

I led Bess into my private library where I kept my most prized possessions. As she entered, I transformed her into a flawless statue. A rare beauty for my collection, to be displayed at next year's Black and White Ball.

Mother®

It wasn't the first playground fight I'd been in, but this one was personal. Another kid made a comment about my Mother® and I flew into a rage. Mother® is important to me. I don't like people talking bad about her.

My Mother® is important to me because I didn't always have one. I was an orphan, or I was, until the anti-orphan campaign was started. I was one of the first to receive a Mother® under the new program.

The Mother® for Every Child program was started by a rich guy at a big tech company. He'd grown up without any parents and didn't want other kids to go through the same experience. He helped design the first Mother® and his company agreed to sponsor the program.

My Mother® does for me all the things anyone else's parent does for them. She reads me books, makes me meals, holds me when I'm sad, sings to me, cheers when I play soccer. She's my Mother® and I love her.

When I'm at school and I'm missing Mother®, I just look over at the school computers. They have an "Intel Inside" sticker on them just like Mother®. It makes me feel like she is there in the room with me.

Some of the other kids don't understand. They got their parents in a different way. That's OK. I'm lucky; my Mother® doesn't get tired or cranky or busy or drunk.

Don't call her a hunk of metal. She's my Mother®.

Puppy

My father was a mortician. He always saw himself as very noble, helping families along during their time of grief. He found a lot of satisfaction in his work.

I, on the other hand, saw a flaw in his work. The person who needed the most help was beyond help. The deceased was the one who had suffered through the agony of death. Who was comforting them? I decided it would be me.

I wanted to find a way to help those who were dying to finish their journey of life happily. Help them be less miserable as they left this world for the next.

The answer came to me when I was at the dentist office staring at the ceiling. To distract patients from the pain of dentistry, there were pictures of puppies pinned to the ceiling.

It all clicked. The first thing I needed was a puppy. Everyone likes puppies.

I picked out a cute puppy from a shelter. It had floppy ears and big brown eyes. I took the puppy home, filled it with poison then headed off to the nursing home.

I found an old man who was terminally ill sitting alone in the corner coughing. I handed him the puppy. He smiled and held the puppy close as it licked him. His face was full of joy as the poison took effect. I'd done it. I'd helped make someone's transition less miserable. I felt a deep satisfaction. It felt good to help those in need.

One. Two. Three.

One. Two. Three. Jump.

Seems easy right? But I'm still here, on the edge of the building… hesitating.

It's the doubt getting in the way, the not knowing for sure. The wondering if you really are working late this time, and not out with him.

I'm not sure what I want the truth to be right now. What if you really are working late, like you said? That would lead to hope. Hope that you have changed your ways. Hope that you do want to be with just me. Hope that I wouldn't have to suffer any more by wondering where you are at night. But there's the catch; hope is not a guarantee, it's a maybe. And it's the months of maybes that have gotten me up here on the ledge.

If I was certain that you're with him tonight, then I could just go ahead and jump and stop suffering. There would be no more obsessing. I would get my life back by giving it up.

But maybe you really are working late and when you're done, you'll show up and hold me close to you and we'll make love in a way that shows how much you care about me. How much you want to be with me. It could be a fresh start for us. The two of us, not the three of us.

One thing is for sure; I should never have dated a married woman.

The safer bet is to go ahead and jump.

Permanent Match

I've always had it, the star tattoo on my left cheek. I was born the year they started the program. Everyone my age and younger had a tattoo on their face. The government had taken over matchmaking.

There were two of each kind of tattoo. Exactly two. Find the tattoo that matched yours and you'd found your mate. Your government approved, genetically selected mate.

Mating with someone beside your approved mate was not allowed. It was illegal and punishable by death.

The problem came that I was in love with Celeste, and she had a tattoo of a fish on her face.

We'd done everything we could do to avoid falling in love but the pull of our attraction was too strong. We'd met in school, the same as both of our parents had before the days of the Permanent Match program. We had smiled at each other a bit during class and things progressed from there.

Soon, we were on the run. Turned in by the guy with a fish on his face, mad that his selected mate was not following the rules. I couldn't blame him really. I'd taken his one and only mate. Without her he would be forced to live a life of solitude, never having a legal love relationship.

During the trial, I tried to take the blame, hoping they would spare Celeste's life. But the judge, who had a star on her face matching mine, selfishly opted to terminate Celeste and let me live.

Therapy

Lena had been coming to see me for about six months. It was obvious from the first session that she had deep childhood issues she was struggling with inside.

Week by week we conversed as I probed deeper into her background. She was resistant to divulge much about herself, leaving me to do most of the talking.

Then, in one of our sessions, I realized something was wrong. A dose of awareness dawned on me. It became clear that I was the patient, not the doctor. All this time I'd been trying to treat Lena when actually she was there to treat me. I was horrified. I'd lost track of who I was. I thought back, looking for memories before my sessions with Lena, but there were none. I felt shattered and lost.

Lena assured me that it was going to be ok. She was there to help. Together we would uncover my memories and help me rediscover who I was.

Our sessions continued. I struggled to find memories of myself. Lena was kind and gentle. I became comfortable with the fact that I was the patient, not the doctor. I looked forward to getting better.

The therapy seemed to be working. I started feeling better about myself. Then one day, Lena said I was strong enough now to know the truth about myself. She held up a mirror so that I could see me. I discovered I wasn't the doctor, I wasn't the patient. I was just the chair.

Pain

The pain had been there as long as I could remember. It was my home. A deep blackness within me that was as much a part of me as my arms and legs. I couldn't remember ever being without it. We traveled together as constant companions.

And then Sara arrived. I meet her at an art gallery uptown where they were displaying some of my works. Large canvases covered with deep blacks and dark browns. Like looking into the abyss.

Sara admired my work although she was the exact opposite of my paintings. She was light and bright with a joyous spirit that danced off her like sunshine. She was kind and confident, and loving…always loving.

We started seeing each other. Dinners, movies and walks in the park. It was unlike anything I'd ever felt. Sara was absolutely amazing. She drew me out into the world.

The more time we spent together, the more my darkness melted. And that was the problem. Before long, I was unable to paint. Without the blackness inside me to fuel my brush, nothing came out of me. I felt lost. I had always painted and now I couldn't paint. I'd been set adrift, rudderless, without my pain to guide me.

The pain had been my home, my second skin. Now it was gone. Sara stole it from me with her love and affection. Desperate, I kissed her then shoved her into the traffic. The darkness returned. I was home. I could paint again.

Firing People

Smash The Hammer: 250-Word Stories

Firing people is one of the more satisfying parts of my job. Every person I fire helps make the company stronger. It disposes of the weak, making room for the strong and efficient.

Plus, it's fun.

I like to play little games with people when I'm firing them. One of my favorites is "The Cookie".

It goes like this. I invite the employee into my office. I wear my quiet, solemn face. They take a seat as I sit at my desk enjoying the worry on their face. I wait a moment, then smile and offer them a cookie. They look relieved, believing something good is going to happen because I offered them a cookie. They take a bite of the cookie and chew for a moment. Then their face scrunches up. Then they say something like "This cookie is stale," and I respond with "Yes, just like you. Time for both of you to go."

I love the moment when their face falls. You can see the shock wash over them as they realize they have just been fired. Sometimes they just sit there with their mouth open. Bits of cookie falling out of it. I have a camera set up for this exact moment. I call it the Trophy Moment.

I have hundreds of these pictures in a large album, like trophies from a safari. I trade them with other bosses who understand the pleasure in firing. It's the small joys like these that make life worth living.

Donna

Today is special. I'm getting out of jail. No more locked in a cell. No more having to do what they tell me. I can do whatever I want.

I will NOT go see Donna.

Gonna be good to be behind the wheel of a car again. To be the one deciding where to go.

When I first met Donna, she worked at the dry cleaner's over on Third. She had the bluest eyes. She wore her hair pulled back off of her face and it made you focus in, right on her eyes.

Looking forward to a Sprite. Been a long time. I remember them as very refreshing.

Donna's day off was Sunday. She'd spend it at the bowling alley. She was a pretty good bowler. She did a little dance when she knocked all the pins down. Even up in the bar, you could see those blue eyes.

First thing I'm gonna buy is a yellow shirt. It's my favorite color. Had to wear just blue for a long time. Had my number printed on it. Really messed up the ensemble.

I remember Donna's pretty feet. She was always wearing shoes that showed 'em off. She had some real tall strappy ones that wrapped around her ankles.

I offered Donna a Sprite once. She refused it. I explained it was very refreshing. She wouldn't even try it.

I will not go see Donna. I will not see what shoes she's wearing. Too much trouble to dig her up.

I Like You

Smash The Hammer: 250-Word Stories

"Wait. Stop for a second. I need to tell you something."

"What?"

"I really like you."

"Oh my God! I knew this was gonna happen. Get off me!"

"Baby, please, can't we just talk about it?"

"Do NOT call me Baby! There is nothing to talk about, Mark. We agreed, no feelings. This was just till the right person comes along."

"You ARE the right person. I love you, Steph."

"Ewww…gross! What kind of person just says that? What is wrong with you?"

"There is nothing wrong with me! I love you!"

"Stop saying that or I'm going to call 911!"

"You're gonna call 911 and tell them what?"

"I'm gonna call 911 and tell them that you're assaulting me."

"I'm not assaulting you!"

"I feel assaulted!"

"Telling you I care about you is not assaulting you; it's the opposite of assaulting you. I don't want to keep doing this without letting you know how I feel about you."

"You broke our deal, Mark."

"I did not break our deal! Our deal was till the right person came along. You are the right person; therefore, I did not break our deal."

"And when exactly did I become the right person, Mark? Was it when I was going down on you? Or maybe when I was spanking your ass?"

"No, it's not like that. You've always been the right person. It just took me a while to realize it."

Technically, I was right, but Steph still got the restraining order.

Ted Nedland

Smash The Hammer: 250-Word Stories

My wife, Kathy, and I had recently moved back to my hometown of Coverton. It wasn't my first choice to move back, but my dad had a job for me at his hardware store and I needed it.

Last Thursday, as Kathy and I drove home from the grocery store, I spotted Ted Nedland, my enemy from ninth grade, walking down the road. I lunged the car forward.

"Look out!" yelled Kathy

"Ted Nedland!" was all I could get out.

Our station wagon bounded over the curb and rushed down the sidewalk, destroying plants along the way. Ted Nedland heard the engine noise and turned to see what it was. I leaned my face forward, wanting to make sure he knew it was me.

And he did. I could see the look of recognition in his face as our station wagon plowed over him. It made a beautiful sweet sound, like ramming a giant water balloon.

I aimed the car back towards the street and continued home. Kathy was in complete shock. Her face drained of color.

"You killed him! Why?" Kathy said, looking at me horrified.

"Stacy Midler," I said, a giant smile on my face.

"What?"

"Stacy Midler. Wasn't that the name of the girl who badgered you all through high school? Ted was my Stacy Midler."

"Oh," said Kathy.

We drove home the rest of the way in silence. As we unloaded the groceries, Kathy asked, "Do you think next weekend we could drive to my hometown?"

The Kim and I

"You're crowding me, scoot over," said Kim.

"Sorry," I said, sliding away from her to the passenger side of the front seat. We sat in silence for a while, each of us leaning against a car door.

When the sun rose and pierced through the front windshield, I asked, "Do you want to get some breakfast?"

"No, don't talk to me," said Kim.

"Jeez, why are you so mad at me?"

"Why am I so mad at you? Look at this place, David! It's a mess. It was your turn to clean up yesterday but there are still food wrappers all over the dash. And your clothes are scattered all over the back seat."

"I'm sorry, Kim. I will make time to clean up today."

"That's what you said yesterday! I've had it! I want to break up. You need to move out."

"I'm not moving out. You move out," I said.

"It's my car, David, so you move out."

"Like hell it's your car. When I had a job, I made three payments on this car, so it's part mine. When you pay me back, I will move out."

"Fine, until then you live in the back seat. I am tired of looking at you," said Kim

"Fine!"

We hung a curtain as a divider and I started living in the back seat. That worked until Kim started bringing dates home. It hurt my heart to listen to them. With no place to go, I moved into the trunk.

Hilda

A taxi driver once told me, "When you meet someone, you know right away why you will leave them." Turns out he was right.

My wife, Hilda, had always been a talker. It was her gift, her passion. When I met her she was giving a speech at the Ladies League. I was there waiting tables. Hilda was stunningly beautiful. The kind of woman that any man would be glad to be with.

When we started dating, I thought about what the taxi driver said. Hilda was a wonderful talker, but it seemed she rarely left moments of silence to be explored. At first I found listening to her charming. Watching her as if observing some beautiful talking painting.

We married in our 20's and set about having a life together. I worked long hours. Hilda kept up with her Ladies League and other causes. Things went along well for years.

Then I retired. I was home all the time with Hilda. Hilda the talker.

I once let a whole week go by where I didn't speak to her. I just nodded now and then and she kept on talking. I finally had enough. The taxi driver was right. The thing I had noticed about her when we met was the reason I needed to be rid of her.

I put the poison in the cup and we sat down to tea. I drank mine slowly, savoring the moment. Hilda chattered on, not noticing I'd expired, finally finding quiet.

To Become King

"Frederick, I trust you understand why I am sending you to the gallows today. You are my son, but as long as you live, I will have no peace. I am constantly on guard making sure you don't kill me in order to become king." My father's face looked weathered, the stress and the worry evident.

It was my 16th birthday. I was sitting in a cold, stone dungeon in my father's castle. My father, King Daniel the II, had become king by killing his father. Now, he was out to make sure that it didn't happen to him.

I was not yet resigned to my fate. I thought maybe I could reason with my father. Promise to renounce the throne and leave the kingdom. I tried talking with him, but he looked at me with cold empty eyes.

I knew then I had a choice. I could let my father kill me or I could take my place as King. I charged forward, catching him off guard. I wrapped the chain that bound my hands around his throat and pulled hard. He fell to the ground gasping for air. "I knew you would kill me," were the final words he spoke before the life ran out of him.

The jailer entered the room. He saw my good father on the ground and came over to help me up. He then knelt before me and said, "Long live the King."

And that is why I've never had any children of my own.

Hotel Lobby

"Take a right here," said Paula.

"I know where I'm going," I said, driving straight past the turn.

"What are you doing? The parking lot is right there!"

"I don't want to park in the parking lot. The parking lot cost seven dollars," I said.

"My God, you're cheap. This is gonna be a great anniversary weekend. You won't even pay seven dollars so we can park. I can't wait to see how crappy the hotel room is."

"The hotel is very nice. Linda liked it fine," I said, as we pulled into an alley where we could park for free.

"I cannot believe you brought me somewhere that you stayed with Linda. You should have just stayed married to that bitch," said Paula.

"Can we stop talking about Linda, please?" I said, turning the car off. I got out and opened the trunk to get our luggage out. Paula got out and slammed her door shut. I took my bag from the trunk and started walking towards the hotel.

Paula grabbed her bag and followed behind me, berating me about not carrying her bag and about taking her to a crappy hotel. By the time we entered the lobby, we were having a full-fledged screaming match.

The patrons turned and watched as Paula and I shredded the last bits of our relationship in the lobby. We broke up right there, vowing to never see each other again, not knowing we were joined by the last available hotel room.

The Closet

We moved to a new house when I was 8. I hated it. There was something in my closet.

The first night we stayed there, I was excited to sleep in my room. Then late at night, I heard sounds coming from my closet. Scratching sounds. I ran and woke up Mom. "Go back to sleep, Steven. I have to work tomorrow," was all she said.

I stayed up all night, in the living room, with the lights on.

The next day, Mom brought home a kitten for me. She said it could sleep in my bed and keep me company.

"I don't want to sleep in my room. Something's in the closet," I said.

"That's just your imagination, sweetie. There is nothing in your closet," she said.

At bedtime, Mom tucked the kitten in with me. It helped having the kitten. Maybe Mom was right. Maybe I'd just been imagining things. I feel asleep with the kitten against my chest.

Around midnight, the kitten started meowing and wouldn't stop. She was by the closet, pawing the door.

I got my lasso and tied one end to my bed and the other around the kitten. I opened the closet a little. The kitten went in, still meowing. A few moments later the meowing stopped. I pulled the rope to get the kitten out. I pulled until I got to the end of the rope. No kitten. Just a frayed end of the rope.

There was definitely something in my closet.

Fat

"You look fat."

Even as I was saying the words, my brain told me to shut up. My whole body tensed immediately, waiting for the coming retaliation.

But it didn't come. All I heard was silence. I opened my eyes and looked at Vivian. She was standing in the doorway of our bathroom, just where she'd been when I uttered the words. Her mouth was hanging open, her eyes staring at me in shock. Her naked body still wet from the shower. She just stood there, not moving. Not moving at all.

"Viv?" I said. There was no response. She was perfectly still, frozen. I got up off the bed and moved towards her. Something was wrong, very wrong.

"Viv, honey, you ok?" I reached out to touch her. Her body was completely stiff. Frozen still. Not cold, but rock solid, like a statue in the park.

I was really worried now. I didn't know what to do. I tried moving her arm but it wouldn't move. She wasn't even breathing. She was just standing there, frozen as if someone had zapped her with a ray gun.

I sat down on the corner of the bed, looking at her. I burst out crying, wondering what the hell was going on.

Then it came back to me. A distant memory. My father talking to me inside his trailer home. I was a teenager and he was passing on his fatherly advice. "Son, no matter what, don't ever call a woman fat."

The Map

I found the map in my sock drawer. Written across the top of it in big bold letters was "Don't tell your Sister".

I followed the map. It led down to a bookcase in our basement. I pulled on the bookcase. It swung out, revealing a hidden door. I knocked three times as indicated on the map. The door swung open. Mom and dad were standing there. Dad grabbed my arm, pulled me in the room and slammed the door behind me.

"Did your sister see you?" he asked.

"No, I don't think so. What's going on?" I said.

"Come sit down, John, and we'll explain," said mother.

The room was decorated really nice. Nicer than the rest of our house. There was a big flat screen TV, two refrigerators, beautiful artwork and expensive furniture.

My parents sat down on the elegant leather sofa. I sat in an electric massage chair opposite them.

Dad spoke. "Your sister will be going through a very difficult time. She turns thirteen next week and will turn into a teenager. Your mother and I think it's best if the rest of us live down here until she is done being a teenager."

"Are teenagers really that bad?" I asked.

"Yes," said my mom. "We've seen the transformation with our friends' children, so we planned ahead and built this room."

"Mom, what happens when I become a teenager?"

"Sweetie, that's a long ways off. You're only nine. We'll worry about that when the time comes."

Old Photgraph

I found an old photograph of us while I was cleaning out the attic. In the photo, we were sitting on the beach on our honeymoon in Hawaii. We looked so happy then.

I remember that day well, waking up cuddled around you on the bed at the hotel. The sounds of the surf outside the room and a peaceful, tranquil feeling. We had all the time in the world.

There were no disagreements that day. No arguing about whose turn it was to take out the trash. No grabbing for the tv remote. No complaining about one another's family or who snored too much.

Relationships are hard work. They start off with so much pleasure and excitement. Everything is easy at first with the focus on the physical, the hand-holding, the kissing, the sex. Each person pumping the other full of endorphins. Each person too high to see the other's shortcomings.

But what goes up, must come down. Before too long the high is not as high, reality starts to chip away at the edge of the fantasy, revealing what has been hidden underneath.

The shift from fantasy to reality doesn't always go well. It can be harsh watching the goddess you fell in love with fall from grace and take shape as the imperfect human being she is.

I looked at the old photograph and cried. I missed the way we used to be. It made me want to go out back, dig you up, and apologize.

Expanding My Horizons

In my thirties, I was on a quest to find "the one". It felt like I'd already dated every woman on the planet. Some didn't like me. And the rest...I didn't like them. So, I expanded my horizons.

I found some plans in a copy of Popular Science and built a transmitter tower in my back yard. Then, I encoded a heart felt singles ad and beamed it into space.

A few weeks later, when I woke up, there was a spacecraft parked by the tower.

Gleeollen had arrived. She was beautiful in her own way. She had purplish hair covering her large head. Purple was always my favorite color.

We hit it off right away. Communication was difficult, but we spent most of our time holding hands. Well, my hand and her suction thingy.

I'd never felt this way about an Earth woman. Gleeollen smiled a lot and wanted to do whatever I was doing. I felt immensely happy when she was around.

After a week, we were sitting on the couch. I made a move to kiss her, but wasn't sure which mouth to kiss. I leaned into the mouth on the left and started to kiss her. She gently shook her head and moved me to the mouth on the right.

Things got hot and heavy and we undressed. When we both had our clothes off, we sat in stunned silence, having found there was no way to mesh our anatomies.

Gleeollen packed up and left.

Will of Alfred Lochner

June 18, 1994

This is the last will and testament of Alfred Lochner. Being of sound mind and body, I leave my family absolutely nothing. There was never a time any of you were there for me and I resent it.

My brother, David, was the worst offender. Not only did he never reach out to help me, he stole the only woman I ever loved, Jessica Norland. David, I've taken the liberty of canceling all your credit cards and ruining your credit. I hope this gives me some joy in the afterlife and causes Jessica to leave you.

To my inept mother, Debra, you may view my personal photo album showing all the important moments of my life and how you were not there for any of them.

To my father, Mort, you did the sensible thing by leaving the family soon after I was born. It shows you were intelligent enough to realize how horrible my brother and mother were. It was your absence from my life that drove me to be a success. I tried to prove that I was worthy of having a father.

To my Irish wolfhound, Trevor, I leave $110 million. Trevor has shown more intelligence and compassion than any member of my family. I trust that he will put these funds to good use.

May you all, except Trevor, burn in hell.

Sincerely,
Alfred Lochner

P.S. If you would like to discuss this further, please feel free to join me in the afterlife.

Re-parenting

At some point in life, you have to stop blaming your parents and do something about the emptiness and loneliness they left you. I was full of broken dreams and unfulfilled promise. Now, I was doing something about it.

I looked through the window at my younger self, sitting by my drunken parents on the sofa. This was my chance to give myself a better life.

Going around to the side of the house, I climbed through my bed-room window, still remembering how to open the latch from the outside with a stick. I waited until young me came to bed and tried not to scare the hell out of myself.

Young me accepted that I was him easier than I thought. Showing him the scar under my eye from falling off the bike when we were seven helped.

I told him he had a choice. He could stay here and fend for himself with our parents or he could come with me and that I would do my best to be the loving, kind parent he needed.

It was an easy choice. We left together. I got an apartment and a job and became a father to myself. I read parenting books and talked to other parents. I set firm limits and expectations. I was loving, kind and patient, things my parents were not capable of being. I parented myself better than they could have. I nurtured my younger self and healed my own pain in the process.

Freedom

I met Linda when I was 25. She was a bit older. Our dating life was carefree and fun, but things changed quickly after we got married. Linda got very possessive.

One night, when I asked her about it, she broke down and told me her previous husband had been a cheater. She said she had never wanted to feel that much pain again.

The next morning my cell phone was gone and the Internet was disconnected. The doors and windows to the house were locked from the outside. Linda had left a note: "I love you, Sweetie! See you after work."

When Linda came home from work, I asked her what was going on. She said she loved me very much and was doing what needed to be done to protect our relationship.

I didn't know what to say. Truth was, she was a lot bigger than me and I was a bit scared of her.

We went on like that for months. Linda leaving for work each day, me at home, feeling more and more isolated.

One night after making love, I told Linda I was feeling really isolated, that I missed getting out of the house and seeing people.

A few days later, after Linda left for work, I noticed the front door was open slightly. I ran out the door towards freedom, elated. Then I saw the 30-foot fence at the end of our driveway.

I wasn't free. Linda had just made my cage bigger.

Ballpark Strange

Smash The Hammer: 250-Word Stories

I was always a big baseball fan. Being at the ballpark on a sunny afternoon distracted me and made me feel better about my crappy life.

Last June, I consoled myself by going to every game I could. Jill and I'd broken up in May, finally ending our three-year relationship.

One afternoon, I got up during the seventh inning stretch and headed to the hot dog stand. As I ordered, a woman next to me rubbed her hand on my arm and said, "I'd like mine with mustard." I looked at her; she was all kinds of sexy. In her 40's, dark hair, green eyes.

I added an extra hot dog to my order.

When the food came, she led me up to the cheap seats where there were few people. We sat and she leaned in close, rubbing her hand on my thigh. When I tried to speak, she put her fingers on my lips.

Next thing I knew we were having sex in the stands while she stuffed both hot dogs in her mouth and mumbled, "Yeah, feed me baby!"

Afterwards, she kissed my cheek and walked away without a word. It was strange.

That became our routine. At each 7th inning stretch, I'd go to the hotdog stand and she'd be there. I'd order hot dogs then we'd head to the cheap seats, have sex, and go our separate ways.

Game by game, the strange became familiar and left me looking forward to next season.

The Clown

On my birthday, my fiancé, Jessica, took me to the circus. It wasn't where I wanted to go on my birthday, but I didn't want to hurt Jessica's feelings, so I went. It was a Friday night and we sat down close by the railing.

I hadn't been to the circus since I was a kid. It was the last place I'd seen my dad. He'd disappeared in the middle of the performance, leaving me alone. I was eight. Jessica didn't know that and I didn't tell her.

The lights dimmed and the show started. A wagon pulled up and ten clowns hopped out. They starting running around, performing gags for the audience.

All except for one clown, a woman, with long bright yellow hair, a red nose, green vest and a top hat with a hole in the top. She stood perfectly still, looking straight into my eyes.

I was mesmerized, enchanted in some way. I couldn't look away. The other clowns moved chaotically, but she moved slowly and deliberately towards me.

When she got to the rail, the clown leaned in and kissed me, soft and slow. "What are you doing?" shouted Jessica, disgusted.

Then the clown held out her pretty hand and I took it. Without a word I went with her and got into the clown wagon where we rode away.

That's when I realized what had happened to my dad. He hadn't wanted to leave me, but the pull of the clowns was too strong.

Terry

Terry was a race-car driver who moved fast. It wasn't just on the track where he moved fast; everywhere he went and everything he did, Terry moved as fast as he could. Walking, driving, talking, eating, or even just taking out the trash.

It wasn't that Terry was in a hurry, he was just trying to stay ahead of his feelings. Those black, sticky, dark feelings from childhood that had been handed down from his mother.

Terry's mom, Margaret, had been single at the time of the birth, having gotten pregnant in the alley behind a bar where she'd been obliterating her pain with shots of Jose Cuervo tequila.

Terry had been her salvation. Before Terry, Margaret had been drowning in the quicksand of her own life. A mess of fears, dark thoughts, resentments, and pain.

When Terry was born, Margaret saw her opportunity. There was this newborn empty vessel. She would take her dark feelings and store them in him. And that's exactly what she did. Starting from the day Terry was born, she told him every dark thing that had happened in her 24 years of life. She removed each feeling from herself and stored them in Terry.

Terry learned early on that if he kept himself busy, he could stay ahead of the dark feelings. That's what led him to become a race-car driver, but at the end of each race, the feelings would be there, waiting for him to stand still in the winner's circle.

Imagining Things

"You're imagining things," said Beth, "There is nothing going on." We'd just left a dinner party at my friend Ryan's house where we'd dined with a small group of people including my younger brother Jack. Beth had seemed very flirty with Ryan.

We climbed into my black mercedes and headed home. Beth reached over to hold my hand. "I love you, Derrick. You are the only man for me. That's why I married you." Her hand was on mine, but it felt cold and machine-like. There was no warmth or love behind her touch.

For weeks, I'd sensed something was wrong, but had no actual evidence of what Beth was up to. That night, after she went to bed, I went downstairs to my lab. I'd made significant progress on my time travel machine the last few weeks, sending small objects a week or two into the future. I thought I could use it to check up on Beth. Climbing in, I set the controls for six months ahead and pushed the button.

When the machine stopped, I got out and went upstairs. There was a newspaper spread out on the kitchen table with the headline "Murdered Inventor Put To Rest". Next to it was a picture of me. The article mentioned the fortune my time machine invention would generate for Beth.

And there, at the bottom of the article, was a picture of Beth. She was holding my brother Jack's hand, both of them smiling at my funeral.

You Would Think

I thought being able to read another person's mind would be great, but it's not. It sucks.

I couldn't always read other people's minds. My ex-girlfriend, Ginny, wished it on me. Bitch. We were in the middle of a fight about me not bringing her flowers when she yelled "Why can't you just read my mind?"…and just like that I could.

Suddenly, I heard every thought she had. It was all there, the thought about whether her face looked fat when she yelled, the thought about how I was an idiot, and the thought about how she couldn't wait to get to work and have sex with her boss on her desk. Yep. Reading someone's mind sucks.

I ran out of the house to get away from her thoughts, but everywhere I went were people. I went into a coffee house to get a latte and was bombarded with people's thoughts. It was overwhelming. I could hear the thoughts of anyone within 20 feet of me whether I wanted to or not.

Out of desperation, I got into my truck and started driving. I had to get away. Someplace with no people. I headed towards the mountains. I drove for three hours until I found a nice secluded place in the woods.

It was peaceful. No people around. While I was setting up a camp for myself, a big brown bear appeared from behind a tree.

The last thought I remember picking up was "This idiot looks tasty."

Monkey Paw

I was standing on the rail of the Golden Gate Bridge, about to jump, when a stranger spoke to me. "Hey, don't jump. I've got what you need."

"What?" I said.

The stranger, a good looking guy, wearing a suit, said "I've got what you need. Don't jump."

"How do you know what I need?"

"Because I once stood where you are, thinking about jumping. I understand."

I hesitated a moment then climbed down and stood next to the stranger.

"I'm Phil," he said, "I brought you a monkey paw."

"A what?"

"It's a monkey paw," he said, holding it out to me. "It's got one wish left and I want to give it to you."

I took the monkey paw and looked it over. "What if I don't believe in wishes?"

"Doesn't matter. Still works," said Phil.

I turned and looked down at the water, considering my options. When I turned back, Phil was gone. I thought for a moment that I'd imagined him, but the monkey paw was there in my hand.

Maybe that was what I needed. One big wish to turn my life around. What to wish for? Cars, women, houses? What would make me happy?

Hmm…happy, that's what I really wanted. I wished for permanent happiness, and I got it. I felt happy all the time. I always smiled, even when my new wife died in a car crash.

That's how I got to this room at the institution. I'm happy to be here.

It Happened Again

It happened again. I knew then, it was me. My brother cut in line. I had a vicious thought then he kind of sizzled and fell over. Just like the day before when Kevin Dinken hit me in the head with a basketball. I got mad and he fell over right where he was standing.

I didn't know what was going on, but I knew I had to learn to be very careful about what I thought. I was really afraid that if I got mad at my girlfriend, Cindy, I would fry her. That would be bad. It wasn't easy for me to get a girlfriend.

That night at home, my parents were distraught about my brother Josh. He was their favorite. I didn't really miss him. He was never very nice to me and constantly reminded me I was adopted. I resisted asking if I could have his room which was larger than mine. Thinking it was better to give it some time.

Controlling my thoughts was harder than I expected. Before long, I'd fried a teacher and both of my parents. I stayed away from Cindy. Trying to keep her safe.

Soon, I stopped going to school and moved into my parent's bed room. It was the largest and had a view. When I needed money, I'd get it from someone walking alone on the street. I felt a little bad about frying people I didn't know, but remembered Mom always said "Use the gifts you're given".

Candy

My dad's name was Jack. He was a boxer and plenty tough. He wasn't afraid of anything, except getting old. He worried what would happen when he was too old to get his way by punching someone in the mouth.

At some point Jack realized having kids was the answer to his problem. He married Raquel, my mom, and started having babies. Three babies, me and my two older brothers Carl and Kenneth. All born in a span of three years.

Starting young, Pop taught us how to defend ourselves. He had his own special method of toughening us up. Once a month, he'd line us up in the living room and throw a single piece of candy onto the floor. If you wanted the candy, you fought for it. It was the only way to get candy at our house.

I was seven the first time I won the candy. I beat the hell out of Carl and Kenneth to get it and its sweet taste made me want more.

After that, I lifted weights and beat up neighborhood kids for practice. Before long I won more than half the candy battles. By age 17, I won every time.

I didn't know it then, but Pop was grooming me to protect him as he grew old. The candy evolved into a monthly check.

Until the day he died, I stayed right by Pop's side, punching anybody in the mouth who didn't like what he said and earning my candy.

Who Wears the Pants?

Larry was never good at standing up for himself. He'd grown up with a controlling mother who made decisions for him and told him what to do. He was 17 the first time he picked his own clothes to wear for the day. His mother, Delores, had been too sick to get out of bed.

Larry found the freedom to choose his own outfit both exhilarating and terrifying. The rest of the day he second guessed his decision, worrying that maybe he'd chosen the wrong outfit.

Two years later, while Larry was attending college and still living at home. Delores announced Larry had a date with Karen, the daughter of Delores's friend.

Karen picked up where Delores left off. At the restaurant, she ordered for Larry and instructed him to change his major to accounting.

A few weeks later, Karen announced their engagement. She planned the entire wedding, even writing Larry's vows for him.

After the wedding, Karen, who didn't want children, told Larry to get a vasectomy, and he did. He never asked himself if he wanted one or not, but in small secret place in his mind he fantasized about making his own decisions.

Then one day he did. He blurted out he didn't want peanut butter and jelly for lunch, he wanted turkey.

Karen was stunned. She immediately called Delores, who came right over.

The two of them together were too powerful for Larry. He did as he was told and got a lobotomy later that day.

Battleground

26 year-old Rick Marshall crouched behind a wall at Blast or Die, the local laser tag venue. He was on the red team and getting shot constantly. Jessica Norwitt, the reason he was here, was on the green team.

Rick and Jessica worked together at Get Your Score Up, a computer game company. Jessica had planned the laser tag team-building event for the staff. Rick worshiped Jessica, but was often too nervous to speak to her.

Rick knew it was a game when he got shot, but felt each hit was one less reason for Jessica to love him. The read out on his laser tag gun showed he currently ranked last.

He saw Jessica run past, her blonde hair up in a ponytail. Rick stood up and shot her in the back. Jessica's vest flashed. She turned around to see who shot her. "Well, well. If it isn't Programmer Rick. I've been looking for you."

"You have?" said Rick.

"You bet. I planned this whole event just so I'd have a chance to get you alone in the dark." Jessica walked towards Rick, a sexy smile on her face. Suddenly, her vest re-activated and she blasted Rick in the chest. "Later, sucker," she said, turning and running off into the darkness.

Rick looked at his gun. The display read "You were destroyed by Hot Jessica". He smiled. Jessica had spoken his name and shot him. In his mind, that qualified him as no longer a virgin.

I've Always had It

I've always had it. I thought of it as a gift, but the older I got, it seemed more like a curse.

My gift first appeared during high school, when I charmed the pants off of Gretchen Hielden during a party where no parents were home. I was 15 and she was a 17 year old senior. I was thrilled to have sex with the most beautiful girl in school, but in the middle of doing it, I knew I didn't love her.

By the end of high school, I added 10 girls to my resume. By the end of college, the number hit triple digits. I could have any beautiful woman I wanted, as long as I didn't love her. That's where the curse part came in. Turned out that if I had actual feelings for a woman, then my charms didn't work.

I consoled myself by adding to my resume. Picking up pretty women wherever I went. That worked for a long time, until I met Marie.

Marie got to me. She was funny, smart, pretty, and had a special something about her. She made me want something I'd never had, a relationship. Because of my feelings, I didn't think she'd go out with me, but she did. We had an amazing date and slept together at her place. I'd finally had sex with someone I actually cared about. I was thrilled.

Turned out Marie was a charmer too, and I was just another entry on her resume.

Tess

"You're too beautiful to be real," I said.

"Yet, here I am," said Tess, sitting down next to me on the sofa.

She was wearing a lovely flower print dress. Her feet were bare and her eyes the most serene color of green. I found her enchanting. When I looked at her, I felt like I was floating in sunshine and that my life would go on forever.

"Would you like some tea?" I asked.

"Yes please. I like the way you make it," said Tess.

I poured two cups of tea then added the lemon and milk. Feeling bold, I leaned in and kissed Tess on her soft neck. She moaned and clutched my thigh. Her lips found mine and we kissed deeply. The heat raged between us.

"I wish you could always be with me," I whispered in her ear.

"Enjoy me while I'm here," she said.

Just then, I heard my wife come home through the front door. Tess quickly stood up and stepped into the painting on my easel.

My wife entered the room and saw me standing by the painting of Tess, brush in my hand. "John, I thought you were done with that one."

"Not quite, Patricia. I've grown rather rather fond of this one. I'm planning on keeping it."

"I don't like it. It's not one of your best. You will sell it with the others."

The next morning, I packed a suitcase and left with the painting of Tess under my arm.

Day at the Office

It was Friday. Last day of work for the week then I could get lost in the weekend.

I worked at Chidler, Chidler, & Chidler, an investment firm. When I arrived that morning, a note on my desk read "Please come see me. D. Chidler."

Don Chidler was my favorite of the brothers. He was a logical guy that made sound business decisions.

I knocked on his door then walked in. "Morning, Mr. Chidler." His office was wood paneled with pictures of him hunting on the walls.

"Hello, Ryan. Close the door and sit."

I sat across from him. His massive mahogany desk between us.

"Ryan, business is slow and we're downsizing."

"I'm getting laid off?"

"No, No. Laying people off is expensive. You're getting downsized."

"I don't understand."

He reached down and opened up a drawer in his desk.

"Ryan, I like you. I'm gonna give you a 10 second head start."

"What?"

That's when I saw it. He straightened up, there was a crossbow in his hands. He pointed it at me and started counting down from 10. I took off running.

I hid in a stairwell and when he entered, I pushed him down the steps. His neck broke when he landed.

When I got home, there was a message on my machine. "You impressed us with the way you handled our big brother. We'd like to offer you his job."

Since then I've learned downsizing can be fun, when you're on the other side of the desk.

Martin

Martin's parents, Patrice and Derek, were concerned. Recently, Seven year old Martin had been showing the signs.

The first sign occurred when Martin found a pencil under the couch. At first his parents thought he was just using the pencil to scribble on paper. They didn't think there was anything to be concerned about, but soon it became evident Martin was writing words. Even worse, he was stringing words together into stories.

There was a history of writing in the family. Patrice's father had suffered from it. He'd tried to quit but couldn't. Finally Patrice's mother packed up Patrice and left, determined to protect her.

Martin's parents took him to the doctor. They wanted the writing cured right away. The doctor gave them restraining gloves. When locked on Martin's hands, they made it impossible for him to hold the pencil.

His parents considered the issue resolved, but inside Martin, stories continued to percolate. The stories filled his head, looking for a way to come out.

One night, Patrice noticed the light on in Martin's room. She peaked in. Martin had the pencil in his mouth, writing stories on the back of his posters. Her first thought was to buy a gag to stop him from writing with his mouth, but she knew, like her father, Martin was incurable.

The next day, Derek built a small shed in back of the house. Martin was allowed to write there as long as he never spoke about it. It became their family secret.

Smash the Hammer

One day when I was about 10, I took my Dad's hammer out of the toolshed and wrapped the handle in leather. I'd just finished reading a Thor comic book and wanted my own magical hammer that I could swing around in a circle to control the rain, thunder, and lightning.

I stood in the middle of our backyard and swung the hammer around and around in a circle. It was sunny outside. I kept checking the sky to see if any clouds were forming. Then on one of the upswings, the hammer slipped out of my sweaty hand and flew high in the air. I lost track of it in the sun. A few seconds later, the hammer smashed down on my head, knocking me out cold.

While I was out, Thor came to me in a vision. He said I was brave and strong, but wielding the hammer was not my destiny.

"What is my destiny?" I asked.

"You John, are meant to be a dentist."

"What? That's a crappy destiny!"

"Ok, how about dancer?"

"Dancer? Are you just making these up?"

"Yeah, kinda," said Thor, "There's no such thing as destiny."

Next thing I knew, my mom was bandaging my head.

Afterwards, I gave up reading comic books. Thor had put me off them. I started doubting there was any grand plan to life.

Over time though, it turned out my destiny was wielding a hammer. I became a carpenter and I was a damn good one.

Family Dog

When my son, Michael, turned five, I got him a dog. A beautiful golden retriever that he named Sampson. I had a dog growing up and wanted my son to have the same joyful experience.

Michael and Sampson bonded. Sampson slept in Michael's bed every night and waited by the door each day for Michael to arrive home from school. They were happy companions.

A couple years later on Christmas Eve, we were eating dinner when we heard tires screech followed by a thud and a yelp. Michael ran outside to see what had happened. Sampson lay in the street mangled. A car raced away down the block.

Sampson was hurt bad. Michael started crying then got down close to Sampson and hugged him. Sampson licked his face. Two best friends not wanting to say goodbye.

We buried Sampson in our back yard that night. I took off his collar and gave it to Michael. He cried himself to sleep while clutching it.

The next morning, although we weren't really in the mood for it, we opened Christmas presents. I'd gotten Michael the magic set he'd asked for. He thanked me and went to play with it.

Later, I found Michael in the yard. He'd dug up Sampson, and somehow used the magic set to bring him back to life.

Unfortunately, the magic didn't fix Sampson's mangled body. I paid the vet to put him back to sleep. Afterwards, I threw away the magic set.

We never got another dog.

Large Coffee, Cream, Seven Spendas

I'm not a Starbuck's guy, but the coffee machine was broken at Bennie's so I headed across the street. I got in line behind a blonde who was six inches taller than me. She had the word "Fate" tattooed on the back of her neck.

I was checking my phone when the blonde ordered. "Large coffee, cream, seven splendas." It caught my attention. It was what I always ordered.

While she put her change away, I ordered. "Large coffee, cream, seven splendas."

"Hey, that's my order," said the blonde.

"It's what I always get."

"Really? How bout that." A smile crept across her face.

"I'm Darrel," I said, sticking out my hand. Her smile instantly vanished.

"Sorry, I've already had a Darrel in my life." She grabbed her coffee off the counter, turned and walked away.

I was intrigued. I grabbed my coffee and walked after her.

"I've never been written off just because of my name," I said to her back.

She kept walking.

"What about fate?" I said.

That got her. She stopped and turned around. "Ok, Mr. Fate, how bout this?" She pulled her shirt up, exposing her stomach. There was a bold tattoo with the words "I hate Darrel".

"Hmm…bad breakup?" I said.

"Yep."

We gave it a shot anyway. We dated and a year later we got married. I could always tell though when Kelly was mad at me. She'd wear something that left her belly exposed. The message came in loud and clear.

Rainy Day

It was raining outside. Dark clouds kept the sunshine out, causing Mark to oversleep.

Then his phone buzzed. There were two texts. One from work, asking why he was late. The other from Rhonda.

Work he could deal with. Mark often talked his way out of being late. Rhonda though was a problem. She had a way of making Mark feel small and worthless. She had been hard to escape. He couldn't let himself get involved again.

Mark read Rhonda's text. "Knock, Knock". Just as he finished reading it, there was a knock on his apartment door. His heart pounded. It was her. She'd found him even though he'd moved without telling her.

Mark had one thought, Run! He jumped out of bed, pulled on some underwear and stepped out on the balcony. It was raining hard. He grabbed the railing, and leapt over to the ground 12 feet below.

When he landed, a bone in his right ankle snapped. He screamed out, but knew he had to keep going. Mark dragged himself along the ground towards his car. When he got close to his Honda Civic, he could see that all four tires were flat. He was trapped.

"Hey, silly boy," he heard from behind him. "Looks like someone needs a ride."

Mark looked over his shoulder. It was Rhonda. She opened her mouth and sprayed him with sticky guilt about never calling her. He felt it pull him in. Once again he was caught in his mother's web.

On the Prowl

Manual was a bachelor who was always on the prowl for a good looking woman. He'd had many love affairs in his lifetime, but nothing lasting more than a few days. He lived by the advice his father gave him, "Don't ever let a woman trap you. Always keep your freedom". This advice was given on their front porch, right before his dad left his mother.

When he got older, Manual lived at the Golden Sunset Retirement Home. Age did not slow his desire, he still loved the ladies. The lady he had his eye on was Doris Fenchment, the hot widow, who just moved into unit 7A.

Manual studied her from afar for a few days. Then one morning, he leaned against the candy machine in the hallway and waited. Doris came by at 9:30 to get her morning snickers. Before she could put money in the machine, Manual held out a snickers with his best smile.

Doris said, "Thank you," then took the snickers from his hand and headed to her room. This happened five days in a row. Then on the sixth day, Doris looked over her shoulder and said, "Aren't you coming?" Manual smiled and followed along to her room.

They made love three times that day before Doris sent Manual on his way. He asked to see her again. "I'm a new widow," she said, "I need to play the field a bit before I commit to anything."

Manual nodded, understanding all too well.

From Nothing

There she was sitting in a booth at the back of the restaurant, laughing and joking with some friends. I forgot to breathe. It was the first time I'd seen her since high school…and she looked amazing.

All those feelings came rushing back, the longing, the fear. The failure of never asking her out, of not giving her a clue of how I felt.

I turned to leave and bumped into the waiter. His tray of chocolate fondue crashed to the floor.

A hush came over the restaurant as everyone turned to look. "Albert, is that you?" I heard her say from across the room.

"Hi, Carrie."

She got up from the table and walked over to me. "Oh my God, Albert, I can't believe it's you!" she said, using a napkin to wipe chocolate sauce off of my jacket.

"I'm surprised you remember me."

"Of course I remember you, we sat next to each other in Algebra class, and I had a huge crush on you."

"What? You had a crush on me? Why didn't you ever say anything?"

"I was shy then. I thought you wouldn't like me."

"Wow. I never knew."

Carrie took a deep breath. "Do you want to go on a date with me?"

I opened my mouth and tried to speak. Nothing came out. Still tongue tied after all these years. I grabbed a napkin and wrote "YES!" in big bold letters. I held it up to her.

We've been married 37 years.

About The Author

Sean Hill is a writer, speaker, and coach.

He was overexposed to a potent combination of Twilight Zone and Monty Python as a child. This lead him down a dark path from which he never fully recovered and bound him with a passion to storytelling.

Sean has spent much of his life combining creativity with work. Starting at age 19, he designed and programmed award-winning video games until he discovered improvisation, where ideas could be expressed as fast as they could be thought.

He is the Founder of the Hideout Theatre, the premier venue in Austin, Texas, for helping people expand their creativity through the study of improv comedy, storytelling, and the art of creating in the moment.

In 2009, Sean combined his love of writing and technology by creating @VeryShortStory, a Twitter feed where over 100,000 followers read the short stories he creates in 140-characters.

When not writing, Sean coaches people to reach their goals and teaches workshops about creativity, communication, collaboration, and innovation skills.

Sean lives happily in Austin, Texas, with his wife, four children, and a lot of dogs. He can often be found performing improv comedy around town with his friends.

CONNECT WITH SEAN ONLINE:

WEB
www.seanhill.com

TWITTER
twitter.com/sean_hill

FACEBOOK
facebook.com/sean.hill.writer

LINKEDIN
linkedin.com/in/veryshortstory

www.ingramcontent.com/pod-product-compliance
Lightning Source LLC
Chambersburg PA
CBHW072011170626
46813CB00005B/2106